My Grandad can draw anything

He can draw
churches,
lurchers,

and the beautiful bark
on silver birches.

He can draw a marching band.

He can draw Andy,
a very handy handyman.

He can draw a cat on a witch's broom,

a very charming bride and groom,

and portraits with eyes

that follow you round the room!

He can draw aeroplanes coming in to land.

A beautiful camel in a land full of sand.

... it's bound to have a "wobbly" hand!

It really really, must be said,
Grandad is SO talented.

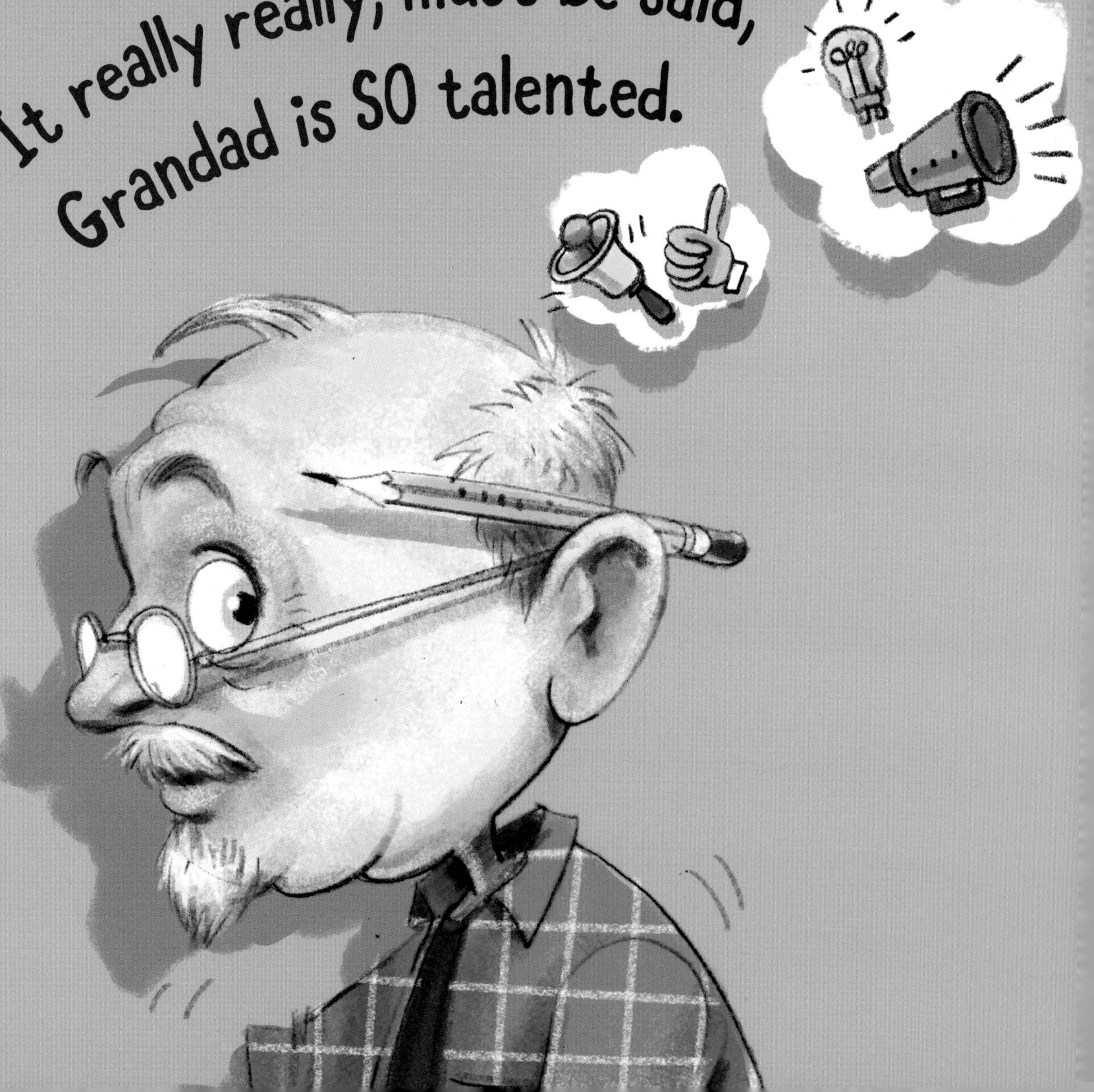

He can draw things from his head!

But now, I'm afraid,
I must make a stand.
He simply can't draw
a left or right hand.

Grandad's drawings are the best you've seen; the finest art there's ever been.

By Royal Appointment an

Invitation to the Palace

Which is why he was commissioned to draw the Queen!

He has, after all, a reputation to save.

Grandad had a scream and shout,
and a little run about.

Side by side
together
we ...

... draw what he loves, elephants, rockets, lovey-doves,

and people wearing oven gloves!

My Grandad can draw anything,
but still,

The Hubble & Hattie imprint was launched in 2009, and is named in memory of two very special Westie sisters owned by Veloce's proprietors. Since the first book, many more have been added, all with the same objective: to be of real benefit to the species they cover; at the same time promoting compassion, understanding and respect between all animals (including human ones!)

Our new range of books for kids will champion the same values and standards that we've always held dear, but to the adults of the future. Children will love these beautifully illustrated, carefully crafted publications, absorbing valuable life lessons whilst being highly entertained. We've more great books already in the pipeline so remember to check out our website for details.

Other books from our Hubble & Hattie Kids! imprint

9781787111608

9781787112926

9781787113060

9781787113077

9781787114302

9781787113121

9781787115156

9781787113862

9781787114180

www.hubbleandhattie.com

First published October 2019 by Veloce Publishing Limited, Veloce House, Parkway Farm Business Park, Middle Farm Way, Poundbury, Dorchester, Dorset, DT1 3AR, England. Tel 01305 260068/Fax 01305 250479/email info@hubbleandhattie.com/web www.hubbleandhattie.com ISBN: 978-1-787115-15-6 UPC: 6-36847-01515-2 © Neil Sullivan, Steven Burke & Veloce Publishing Ltd 2019. All rights reserved. With the exception of quoting brief passages for the purpose of review, no part of this publication may be recorded, reproduced or transmitted by any means, including photocopying, without the written permission of Veloce Publishing Ltd. Throughout this book logos, model names and designations, etc, have been used for the purposes of identification, illustration and decoration. Such names are the property of the trademark holder as this is not an official publication. Readers with ideas for books about animals, or animal-related topics, are invited to write to the publisher of Veloce Publishing at the above address. British Library Cataloguing in Publication Data – A catalogue record for this book is available from the British Library. Typesetting, design and page make-up all by Veloce Publishing Ltd on Apple Mac. Printed in India by Parksons Graphics